PUNKY
ALOHA

PUNKY

Dedicated to my three.
Teisa, Ehukai, and Keali'i: my wind, my sail, and my stars.

Punky Aloha
Copyright © 2022 by Shar Tuiasoa
All rights reserved. Manufactured in the United States.
No part of this book may be used or reproduced in any manner whatsoever without written permission except in the case of brief quotations embodied in critical articles and reviews. For information address HarperCollins Children's Books, a division of HarperCollins Publishers, 195 Broadway, New York, NY 10007.
www.harpercollinschildrens.com

ISBN 978-0-06-307923-6

The artist used a drawing tablet to create the digital illustrations for this book.
Typography by Chelsea C. Donaldson
22 23 24 25 26   PC   10 9 8 7 6 5 4 3 2 1

❖

WOODSON

ALOHA

Shar Tuiasoa

HARPER

An Imprint of HarperCollinsPublishers

Hi, I'm Punky!
Punky Aloha.

That's the nickname my grandma gave me.
She is my best friend, and we do *everything* together.

Grandma calls me
her brave adventurer,
which I am *now* . . .

but I wasn't before.

The truth is I wasn't always brave.
Making new friends? Now THAT was hard.

Don't believe me? Well, let me tell you
about the time I had to go on a very
important but very scary adventure.

It all started with **banana bread.**

And not just any banana bread. I'm talkin' about Grandma's famous, fresh-baked, bananas-from-the-backyard, warm-from-the-oven banana bread.

"Punky! We're out of butter,"
Grandma yells from the kitchen.

If I know one thing, it's that you can't have Grandma's banana bread without butter melting right on top. Kimo's Market just so happens to make the best butter on the island.

"I need you to pick up the butter today. I can't come this time, but you got this."

"You mean, you want me to go ALONE?" I cried. "B-b-b-ut if I go to the market, I'm sure to bump into someone new. And whenever I bump into someone, I start to feel shy."

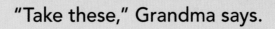

"Take these," Grandma says.

"They're my magical
brave glasses, for brave
adventurers like you."

"Brave glasses? There's no such thing! How do they work?" I ask.

"Just put these on anytime you feel nervous or shy and they will help you feel brave."

"Are you sure?"

"Of course I'm sure. I use them all the time."

"And Punky, do you remember how we share our aloha?"

"Be helpful.
Be giving.
Be brave.

This is how we share our aloha," I recite.
"Well, all right!" Grandma smiles.

I know I gotta go. The banana
bread depends on it—on me.
But as soon as I step outside
the gate, I hear it, a loud . . .

"OINK OINK OINK"

"A little help? Please? I've got all these mangoes I need to take back to my family," the pig cries.

OINK OINK

I can feel the glasses working.
I get just enough courage to remember:

Helpful . . .
giving . . .
brave.

Share your aloha, Punky.

"We can put the mangoes on my skateboard if you want," I say shyly.

"What you did was very helpful. Thank you so much," the mommy pig says as she nods to her piglets.

One of them trots up to me and gives me a flower lei.

I have a funny, warm feeling inside. I kinda like it. I thank them,
grab my skateboard, and head for the market again. Then I hear . . .

BZZ
BZZ

"Why are you so sad?" I ask.
"I'm not very good at being a bee. I didn't collect *any* pollen for the hive, and I'm too embarrassed to go back empty-handed," the bee buzzes.

BZZ BZZ Bzz Bzz

I adjust my glasses and smile. *Be helpful. Be giving. Be brave.*

"Here. Use my lei. It has plenty of pollen!"

"Really? Thanks! Um, uh, wait here!" the bee says.

"I don't have much to give you, but this honey is fresh, straight from the hive!"

Fresh, gooey honey. My favorite!

I start to feel like making new
friends doesn't have to be scary.

In fact, it could be downright yummy.
Maybe Grandma's brave glasses really *are* magic.

When suddenly . . .

CRA

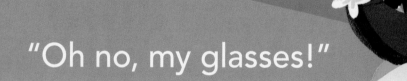

"Oh no, my glasses!"

It looks like he needs my help! The glasses are gone, but I can still use my aloha.

"How's this? My grandma rubs honey on my scrapes to keep them clean," I say. "And sometimes there's even extra."

YUM!

"Wow! That *does* really help. Thank you—"

"Punky. I'm Punky Aloha."

"I'm Kai, and I'm sorry about your glasses."

"That's okay. I don't think I
need them anymore."

"Well, just in case, my dad might
have some tape at his store. He
owns the corner market."

"Wait, your Dad is Kimo?"

"Yeah, why?"

I giggle as we both jump on our
skateboards and head to the market.

KIMO'S

"Dad! This is my new friend . . ."

"Punky!" Kimo says. "Aloha! It was kind of you to help Kai. That must've taken a lot of bravery. Look here: I have some fresh butter for your grandma. I know how much she loves this stuff."

After I wave goodbye to my friends, I race home with the butter in my bag and my heart full of courage.

"Grandma! Grandma!"

"I went on a really big adventure!
I made new friends by being brave
and helpful, just like you told me!"

"See? I'm so proud of you.
My brave Punky Aloha."

Now, I don't know everything, but I do know this:
That day I became a brave adventurer.

And it all started with **fresh-baked banana bread.**